W9-AXX-340

Disney
ALICE
in
WONDERLAND

Curiouser and Curiouser

Published by Creative Edge, LLC, 2010, an imprint of Dalmatian Press, LLC, Franklin, Tennessee 37067.

Printed in China

10 11 ZHE 10 9 8 7 6 5 4 3 2 1
CE12819

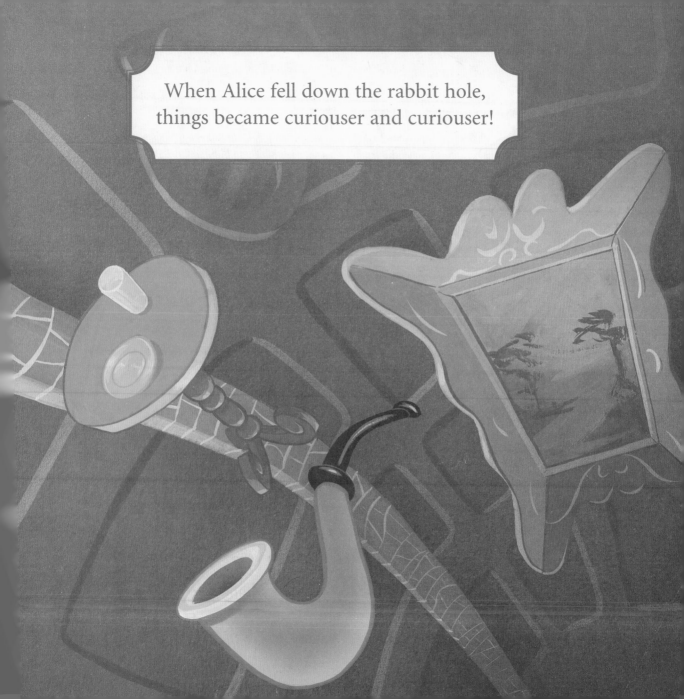

When Alice fell down the rabbit hole,
things became curiouser and curiouser!

Most peculiar!
Odd creatures in a pool of tears!

Just a bit silly!
A Walrus and Carpenter coaxing oysters.

How absurd!
Alice sprouts up in a house!

Very extraordinary!
A garden of talking flowers!

Strange, indeed!
Tea for three—served up with foolishness.

Quite unusual!
A Cat atop a Queen at croquet!

Oh, wonderful!
A door with a talking Doorknob!
Will it take Alice home?

Or was it all just a wonder-filled dream?